After This. . .!

T. E. Williams

T. E. Williams

After This...!

Dedicated to Barbara & John Ray

T. E. Williams

Chapter 1 "Clothes Are Temporary"

In the summer of '73, I sat with my Mother listening intently to the summer birds out back. We often sat at the picnic table, which was some distance in the back of our home watching for the red robin who frequently came to visit her. My Mother had the gift to summon birds. She had the unique ability to have a woodpecker echo the faint knocking of her own sound. She knocked out a beat with her skinny knuckles, and in the distance you could hear the woodpecker mimic her exact tune.

The rust-colored picnic table was weathered and worn. As a 5 year old, I was easily impressed by my Mother's unique way of teaching us.

Our picnic table had been used as a stage prop for every Thanksgiving play at the local elementary school. Year after year, my Father would proudly stain the table which had two long benches connected to it on either side. I remember the beautiful cornucopia Mom made which would grace the center of the picnic table which added to the fall theme. Beautiful fall foliage, stalked corn and first fruits filled the cornucopia which sat atop a long white doily which she decorated with small red maple leaves and acorns. The doily ran the length of the table and draped over the sides. The principal was always impressed when he requested the table.

My parents were very sociable and civic-minded, hosting parties and serving cocktails. My mother could often be seen in her white cocktail dress along with Mary, our maid running from guest to guest making sure their drinks were topped off. My Mother was very active at the elementary school. PTA, Auxiliary Committee and trip chaperone. Mary was great. She introduced us to macramé, pottery and origami. She taught me how to meditate. In the evenings, she'd actually ring the tiny dinner bell.

My Father would either be on the grill or standing in the center of the other dads who were seated around. He'd steal the spotlight with one of his stories. He was a hardworking Auto Mechanic, and fought in the Korean War; a true jack-of-all trades. He was a Master Welder. At the end of each story, all the dads would laugh out loud, slap their knees and throw their heads back roaring as they pat him on the back. My Father laughed with his shoulders and had the whitest teeth. He is the only dark man I'd ever seen with blue eyes. He knew how to keep them entertained. They all drank Miller beer or scotch whiskey, smoked cigarettes and played pea knuckle until the food was ready.

The parties would last into the late evenings and Daddy would turn on the back porch lights to keep the party going. The sound of music was always bellowing from the speakers he mounted at the corners of the back porch. It was a fine time.

Most of our neighbors didn't look like us. They were always inquiring when my Father was going to throw his next shindig. Not because the cars would be lined up and down Stuyvesant, or because the music would disturb them, but because Jack and Donna Marshall threw the best parties in Hiltonia. The neighborhood children played while waiting to toast marshmallows, but not me. I was always near Mommy.

There were 6 children in my family, 4 girls, Monica, Margie and Michelle; 2 boys, Mark & Mike. And me; I'm the 'baby'. My position was solidified by the fact that all of the children were in school today and I was home with Mommy and Mary. Mother worked at the school both as a Crossing Guard and in the cafeteria. When she came home, it was our time, just her and me.

Occasionally, she would hoist me onto her back along with her tennis racket and go down to the park to play wall ball. We had adventures as we hiked through the large gully en route to the courts. When we'd walk we would identify trees, birds and types of flowers. The park had fences with deer, geese and peacocks behind them. The chestnut trees were preparing to ripen for the fall season. Cadwalader Park had paddle boats which would circle the large lake that had an island in the middle. I loved the large white rocks and bright red benches. It had a sort of Norman Rockwell feel to it. Everything outdoors was a new lesson. Mommy would see the balloon man at the East exit who she would occasionally buy a red balloon from just for me. We climbed crab apple trees together and when it was time to come down, she'd hold out her arms and I'd jump from the lowest branch into her arms. Mother absolutely loved the outdoors. After tennis we would stop by the swings.

But not today.

Today we are in the backyard waiting for her special friend, the red robin. As Mary called from the back door, Mom told me to continue to wait while she took a phone call. Mary was almost 6 feet tall and was afraid of my Mother who stood a shapely, small-waist 4 foot 10 inches! Dad called her 'doll face'. He said it this morning as he kissed her goodbye. It was never the same kiss. I remember seeing her neck as her chin slanted up to receive it; her eyes closed as if her lips tasted sweet berries.

She was bathing me in the tub. He kissed my forehead and left. Mommy grabbed me up in a fluffy towel and carried me to her room. I begged Mommy if I could wear what she called my 'sun suit'. It was a yellow and white haltered one-piece girly girl outfit with ruffles on the bottom. I felt incredible in it. I remember smiling as she tied the yellow straps at the back of my neck.

Mary made chicken noodle soup for lunch. I can smell it from the kitchen window where she placed it to cool. Mom and Mary can see me from the kitchen window, but weren't looking. They hadn't seen me get down from the picnic table and remove my 'sun suit', socks then panties rolling around in the sand. It was *freedom*. My Mother dropped the phone and ran with a sheet from the clothes line, "Nooo! MISSY I'm surprised in you!" She said beckoning me to her. Mary stood with her hand over her mouth in the doorway exclaimed, "My stars! Ms. Donna, what's going on?"

My mother shaking her head from side to side as she ran to me and wrapped me up in the soft pretty smelling white sheet Mary just hung an hour ago. "What are you doing?" she exclaimed. I felt ashamed due to their reaction, and not because of my nakedness. "I want to feel the sand on me!" My Mother snatched me and my panties up in one fell swoop and into the house slamming the screen door.

My Mother explained that it was not appropriate to be outside without any clothes on. I understood, though I had questions which I would never ask. I began to cry. "I want to feel the sand on me Mommy! I just wanted to feel the sand!" The warm pink sand was all over the back yard with the exception of the area of the picnic table where grass grew. We sat and ate cooled chicken noodle soup together and she put my 'sun suit' back on me.

As school began in September, I was to become a new morning Kindergartener. There was also afternoon Kindergarten but my Mother said that it was our special time, so I was able to leave with my sisters and brothers for school but Mommy would pick me up at noon. Mommy dressed me in a red and white top with red pants. She played tennis in the park until school was over at noon. She picked me up hoisting me onto her back piggy style as we bounced all the way home.

Down the street at a neighbor's home lived my Mother's friend Ms. Shari who had a little boy in Afternoon Kindergarten. His name was Evan. Evan was a 'bad little boy' who was always in trouble. As the grownups sat drinking coffee at Shari's, Evan and I would play all sorts of games, Spy, Hide-n-Seek, Cowboys & Indians, we would even play school. Ms. Shari had an attic that had pictures which were very different than the pictures in our home.

Evan showed me a poster of all the Disney dwarfs engaged in all kinds of sexual acts with a bare breasted Snow White. She looked so pleased. I couldn't stop looking at the poster. It had shattered everything I had come to know about Disney and innocence. Evan and I invented a game we called 'Closet'. In the closet we'd take off all our clothes. That was the game. I liked to feel Evan on my skin. It was the best game ever.

One day, Evan lifted his parents' mattress and showed me his Father's gun. It was black with a white handle. He said one day it would be his. Every day while Mommy and Ms. Shari talked at her kitchen table Evan and I were playing 'Closet'.

My Sister Monica who was already a teenager at that time wanted to surprise our parents by taking me down town to get my portrait taken with her first check. She had been working at Sears and earned enough for the portrait. Monica was a very quiet, congenial young lady. She put the prettiest purple dress on me, white shoes and ribbons and gave me two pony tails.

We caught the Mercer Metro down town. I loved bus rides and especially loved to be with Monica. She would let me pull the rope that alerted the driver to stop. This ride however, was uncomfortable, mostly because the underwear she chose for me was too tight. They belonged to my sister Michelle who was a string bean. I told Monica I wanted to take them off. As the bus arrived down town, I screamed, "My panties are too tight!" Monica hushed me with her finger to her lips.

We exited the bus and I stood on the corner of East State and North Broad bellowing! "My panties are too tight!" Finally, as a grand gesture, I reached under my purple dress, stepped out of the frilly ruffled panties and handed them to her! "TOO TIGHT!" Poor Monica was so embarrassed she snatched me up under her arm and proceeded to the portrait studio. It was the best photo I have ever taken and my parents were quite surprised. No mention was ever made about the 'State & Broad' panty incident.

Michelle and Margie were close in age, Irish twins. My Mother dressed them alike, did their hair the same and they also shared a room. It was decked out with twin beds with the same comforter and pillow set and curtains on each window which matched the set. They had watermelon colors.

I had my own room which was red and white. I had bunk beds and a bureau. Michelle was very reserved and shy. Margie was just the opposite. Margie taught us to read, ride bikes, climb, swim, blow bubbles, sew, iron, and how to fight. Margie liked to fight, especially for me and

Michelle. She would dare anyone in the neighborhood to challenge us. She'd stand behind me holding my hands in a fighting stance and swing my arms to and fro. Michelle did not like to fight. But Margie said she would have to someday.

Michelle was Daddy's girl. She'd always be on his lap or on his broad shoulders. They always played 'Guess which hand it's in'. My brothers were hardly ever home. They always had some kind of practice for sports. When they were home we always played wrestling. Mike was the older brother and Mark was between Monica and Margie.

Although I had many sisters and playmates, I loved to be alone and naked. I was 10 years old when I found what I called my 'Magic Button'. I would play with my 'Magic Button' anywhere; in the bathroom, in my bed, even in the living room, as long as nobody was around. My 'Magic Button' would make me go to another place where new sounds would enter into my mind, fluffy white clouds would appear and my head would go backwards into my pillow. My 'Magic Button' was the best toy I could hope for. I would reach into my panties, find just the right spot to turn it on and go to the happiest place on Earth!

As a 4th grader, Mommy began a full time job and told me I had to use the house key she placed around my neck to let myself in every day. I would rush home from school, lock the door, take off all my clothes and play with my 'Magic Button'. I didn't want anyone to be around and I certainly didn't want to share the great secret. With a house full of children and their friends, it was the only thing I had for myself. We shared everything we owned.

I played in the mirror, so I can see what it looked like. It was soft and pink. I noticed that there was certain things I can make with it, up, down and just below it I can use something cold on it and it wouldn't bother me. I can go inside it. I would come home and look around to see what cold things I can use. I used ice cubes, popsicles, my Dad's metal hammer, a butter knife and my Atari joystick. I'd use a cucumber and sometimes I'd even rub myself onto the corner of the dining room table! This thing was endless! I hated when my sisters and brothers came home because I knew my 'Magic Button' game would be over and I would have to put my clothes back on.

Monica had met and married a guy named Paul. She moved to where her husband lived in Connecticut. Our Mother was originally from Stamford. Monica had a baby boy they named, Patrick. We all missed them very much, but we would get to visit her in the summer.

The summers were great with Monica. Her husband was a nice young man with unique features. He treated us well. He worked every day and Monica would stay home with us and with the baby. She played her music for us. She played Stevie Wonder, the Commodores, Jackson 5, the Brothers Johnson, Ohio Players, Bootsie's Rubber Band and the Emotions on her HiFi. Sometimes she would play West Indian music. It was cool. We would have talent shows right in her living room. We made up dances off 'Love Will Keep Us Together', and 'Stop in the Name of Love'. We would play outside on the massive rocks she had in the back of her cul-de-sac.

One day while playing in her room I found a magazine with naked people. It was fascinating! I liked the different size breasts and skin colors on the ladies. I thought to myself, 'I'm not the only one who likes to be naked!' I played on their bed with my 'Magic Button' while looking at the magazine. After some time I heard something I'd never heard before. It was the sound of an 'Ooze', and I felt bubbles come out of me. As I brought my fingers up to see what it was, I saw it looked like rubber cement from art class with a stream of blood going through it. I felt ashamed. My button was soft now and I wondered if it would ever come back. I put my clothes on.

I didn't want Paul to see the magazine with the ladies so I ripped the breast out of each page. This was just for girls to see. I remember thinking, 'Boys should definitely not be seeing this stuff'. The magazine should not be sold to just anyone, after all it was Monica's magazine, so I thought. I put the magazine under the bed and went to play outside.

Monica later called me from outside to discuss what happened to her husband's magazine. I couldn't explain it, but I was shocked that it was *his* magazine and never looked at him quite the same.

T. E. Williams

Chapter 2 "Boys are Stupid"

When the summer ended, and we were headed back to Jersey, I remember all the lush greenery that would greet us coming down Stuyvesant. It was absolutely beautiful. I longed to see Mommy and Daddy and reconnect with 'The Club' (neighborhood boys). I wanted to sleep in my own bed.

This particular summer we came back the neighborhood boys said I changed. I was their friend when we left and when I come back they said I'd changed. What changed? I can still whoop all their butts and if I couldn't, then Margie could! I had taken actual blood oaths with most of them and they all swam in my pool! Who did they think they were? I could outride, out climb and outrun any of them! I could even hit a homerun over the fence! Half the boys in the neighborhood couldn't do THAT! These are the guys I play H O R S E with and I had a mean jumper.

One day we were all out in the front yard getting wet by the hose. My bikini was green & yellow. Michelle's was orange & red. Margie's was blue & white. The boys came down on bikes and were pointing and laughing and we didn't understand. Later that evening after relay races we were all sitting on Evan's porch eating ice cream and crunching, which was our way of hassling each other as kids do. (Trust me if any kids came from 'Up The Hill', we were down for each other and all bets would be off). But these silly boys on this evening were laughing at ME! I couldn't understand what was so damn funny! Finally I grabbed Evan by the ear and said, "What the heck is going on?!"

He said, "They're laughing because you got titties!" They all joined in a little tune called 'Mitty's got Titties'. They jumped around cupping their hands over their own chests shouting, 'Mitty's got Titties! Mitty's got Titties!' They bobbed up and down like apes and made armpit farts! I hated them! I punched Evan on the arm hard enough to make it frog and stomped all the way home. Where the heck did they come from? Michelle ain't have none! Margie always had 'em! So what is the big deal? What are they for anyway? I just wanted to be with my friends! We were 'The Club', and I was the leader before I left! I was finally home! Assholes!

I asked my Mother, "Why do we have to have 'em?" She sat me down and explained to me that the sole purpose of having breasts was to produce milk for my young. I screamed, "These things are ruining my life!" She said I may feel differently later. Mom began to tell me about some upcoming changes I did not appreciate or accept.

The next weekend, she was in my room watering my plants and saw red spots on my panties as I was sleeping. I was 10 years old! I couldn't understand all this and I wanted most to be with 'The Club'. I can't be with the boys with all this going on!

Mom was sweet. She bathed me and put a fluffy pink robe on me. She bought me some Stayfree Maxi pads and a sweet little bra with a rose in the middle. I hid the pads far under my bed because she told me it *will* come again. The next time it happened, they were gone from under my bed. Must I share everything?

The summer I turned 13 I was highly anticipating joining the Legionnaires, a local precision drill team for neighborhood teens run by a lady named Mama. Michelle was already on the team. She had taught me everything I needed to know to be a Legionnaire. There were about 40 girls going out, 20 got recruited.

Mama held contests to see who the squad leaders would be. I got 1st squad. But because there were 4 squads and 5 really good leaders, the Captain made me a Guard Arm. She said, "You are small, spicy and NOT shy so you have the privilege of being Guard Arm. She held her head up as she said this. She told me that while everyone else has to be uniform and precise, I can twirl as I wish, move as I wish, and perform as I wish, but I MUST stand out! She gave me a little silver vest, a baton and a shiny blue skirt with silver fringe. Everyone else's uniform skirt was muted blue. We all wore blue cowboy hats with a white feather plume extending out on the right, and white drill boots. I honored the position and we won many competitions which I gladly took credit for. I had become emancipated from my sister because I was in the front of the entire squad! I had become GUARD ARM. My head was too heavy to hold up. I was no longer in Michelle's shadow. Everybody noticed me and for the 1st time, I was so happy that 'Mitty's got Titties'.

That year, the Legionnaires had a huge competition coming in November followed by both the holiday parades through town. There were several places we had practice; 'Down The Hill', white top (a huge white parking lot), down town, Cadwalader Park or the grocery store parking lot. Sometimes we'd practice in the Community Room which was located in the basement of Mama's building.

At practice, we were taught the true meaning and history of being a proud Legionnaire. We learned discipline, unity and self-respect. The community had pride in us and we had pride in each other. Everyone knew the Legionnaires. We empowered each other and encouraged each other. If it got back to Mama that one of her Legionnaires got into trouble they'd get booted off the team with shame. Same honor code went for the drummers. They were like our brothers and they were supposed to look out for us.

We were set for the statewide competition and had intense practices. Mama had sessions on beauty, hygiene and boys. In this forum, we could discuss any issues bothering us as teens. It was all confidential.

Being Guard Arm was making me popular. I felt like the centerfold of that magazine from the past. All eyes on me!

The Legionnaires performed all over NJ, NY and Philadelphia. Even halftime at a Sixer's game.

That summer, there was a block party in the park which all the children in my family attended. We danced and had a great time. The music was blaring 'Must be the Music', 'So Fine', 'Numbers', 'The Art of Noise' and got really turned up when the first note kicked 'TRENTON ROCKS TO THE PLANET ROCK....DON'T STOP!' We would grab anybody and start dancing. People would say, 'Those Marshall girls know how to get a party started!' As the sun was going down, each of us would walk slowly through the park with our conquest for the night. Marshall girls looked good, famous for smarts, small waists and pretty face. We were *gonna* leave with someone.

Unfortunately, we all came home one by one. As we came home, each of us was given the devastating news that our dear Father Jack Marshall had died. It must've been very painful for my Mother to have to tell each of us this news account again and again, each time, breaking down, consoling us individually, one by one. What a bitter taste it held. The Pastors of our church came over, friends we hadn't seen in a while came over and teachers too. Everybody had a dish, a tray or Halo Farm juice. My Father was well loved and of course, he had worked on all their cars. Ms. Shari and Evan came down to our house with 3 boxes of Dunkin Donuts and Halo. She said my Mother shouldn't have to cook. Evan came to me and hugged me. He held me for a long time. I felt myself forgiving him for the past. I think he was enjoying it.

At the funeral, the Legionnaires assisted in Parade Dress attire to contribute to the family and honor our Father. He was a great man. I remember touching my Father's cold face in the casket. It was my first funeral but I didn't cry. My heart pounded as they folded the flag of United States of America and placed it in my Mother's lap. Then I cried. Not for me, but for her. They were soul mates, one for another, and for their children. As we were entering the limousine I looked back as the Legionnaires saluted my Father's casket with unspeakable valor!

The Legionnaires went on to perform for 4 years in the limelight. Endless talent shows, parades, pageants and competitions. As more teens graduated, got pregnant or lost interest, the less we won at competitions. I was juggling high school, cheerleading and Guard Arm. And I missed Daddy. It was time to pass the torch as it had been passed to me. At recruitment, I chose a small, spicy girl much like myself to be Guard Arm to continue the legacy and faded into the back.

After practice for the '82 Christmas Pageant at the Community Room, one of the drummers pulled me to the side, took me in a stairwell and began to kiss me. I liked Barry a little so I kissed back. Barry had a girlfriend and she was on the other side of that door.

He began to pull me down to the floor. This was as far as I wanted it to go. I breathed out, "No" but there was no stopping him. The hallway was dark. I focused on the blinking red EXIT sign, crying. I made no attempt to stop him from what he was doing. He was violating me, but I didn't stop him. I had never been with a *man* before. He tasted salty and hot. The sweat that was so hot leaving his face was cold hitting my shoulder. When it was over, he helped me with my skirt which was all twisted around me. He pushed my hair out of my face and walked out that door. I found Michelle and was quiet walking all the way home. I never said a word.

On the morning of February 1st I woke up 2am and threw up all the spaghetti my Mother made that night. I had never vomited before. I was pregnant. My Mother had Michelle take me down to the clinic and it was confirmed. My pregnancy lasted 3 months and the child aborted itself. I was extremely depressed. Michelle asked who did it but I couldn't tell her. I felt she would be mad at me, and not Barry. Barry and Michelle's friend Vi were going out. I didn't want Vi to find out. I didn't date for the rest of the school year. My grades suffered, I had limited friends and missed lots of drill practice. The popularity of the Legionnaires was fading, I lost my Father and my baby and I couldn't see past it. I cannot believe I used to think boys were so cool. I had learned that boys can be dangerous. I decided to forget about them for the time being.

I got a job at Wesley McNair Daycare Center through the school Co-Op which was set up to assist single parent homes. The program was very enlightening working with the Red Class, which was comprised of ten 3 year olds and ten 4 year olds. Ms. Wright was very good with the children. I would observe everything she did. She made special learning activities for the children, play time, nap time, snack and recess. I threw myself into the work. I truly enjoyed it and had considered teaching as an avocation. I hadn't realized it at the time, but I was transforming.

I had begun to see myself doing it in the future. Looking into the children's eyes, I wanted to protect each of them. The best thing you can do when depressed is take the focus off yourself. Those children looked forward to seeing me every day. I tied so many shoes, colored so many pictures, posted on so many bulletin boards, and wiped so many noses. I realized I was in no way ready to have a child, but was certainly ready to assist with 20. What a confidence booster! They eventually closed the daycare due to lack of participation.

T. E. Williams

Chapter 3 "Smoove as Suede"

By the time my senior year started I had regained my self-esteem. I had a hell of a summer. My body was right and I had the most beautiful hair. My dark skin was still smooth from good living. I had earned enough money to buy a new wardrobe and a car. This was the first year Margie and Michelle would not be in school with me. I felt liberated, independent and confident. The year flew by. I got straight A's. I took classes to propel me into college. Got a 1270 on my SATs and I took pre-placement tests at the Community College for acceptance. I figured I'd take some Liberal Arts classes then transfer to a 4 year college.

I met a nice guy, Julian, a little shy, but a great dresser. He was from a good family and upward bound like me. Julian and I would see each other often. He worked as a janitor in Housekeeping at the local hospital. He intended to join the Army after high school. He wanted to be a jet engine mechanic. I got the impression he was looking for a wife.

Life has a way of changing your plans. I got a job as a Legislative Assistant with a local lobbying firm which hired me full time after graduation. My Mother's children left the nest one by one. She got sick soon after and the house fell into disrepair. Our service was cut off for lack of payment and she had to cook on the kerosene heater that winter by candle light. The roof needed work and when it rained, it rained in my bedroom. Julian and I did all we could to help with the bills and we became very close due to similar home life and circumstances. Julian was a natural born provider and husband-material. He put no pressure on me for sex. We were intimate, kind and tender. He cared about me.

At work, I was responsible for advertising in the Firm's legislative magazine. The magazine was mostly about current bills to be sent to Congress to become laws. The Firm would lobby for/against bills headed out. It was very interesting work. I learned quite a bit about the Assembly and Senate of New Jersey. At the annual conference, I was asked to speak about women in government. Margie and I prepared a speech which Lincoln himself would have given ovation to. It was one of the greatest moments in my life.

As I advanced at the Firm, I began seeing more of Julian. We ate Chinese food in the park because our job sites were in the same area. He was romantic and I needed a man to be. He used to rub my temples. His greeting was to swipe his open palm softly down the center of my face. I would return the gesture. It was our thing. We would talk for hours on our days off. Soon after we finally had enough money to get my Mom's power back on but she became gravely ill. Decisions had to be made as to who would take care of her. Monica eventually moved Mom in with her not too far from our house. The house was put into foreclosure and it was time to say goodbye which was extremely difficult for me to do. Julian was one of 5 brothers in his home. I did not want to move in with him, so I moved with Mom to Monica's apartment. It was a bit cramped but she made us feel as comfortable as possible.

Julian would come by, but we never had any privacy there. I would stay weekends at Julian's Mother's. She was nice to me and saw me as a daughter. She said she was sick of living in a house with men. She was separated from his Father and also worked at the hospital.

Julian worked really hard to provide for both homes and contribute to my Mother's care. He took a second job at a grocery store and promised he would eventually have enough for us to get our own place. I was getting raises often and I had put college dreams behind me, which is why it seemed only natural progression that by that summer I was pregnant with Julian's child. We told everybody. He proposed upon confirmation at the obstetrician as the ultrasound showed us we were having a baby girl. We were excited, yet concerned about the future.

Julian was very supportive. He talked again about joining the military so that we can have a good foundation. He suggested I move in with his Mother so she can monitor and assist me with the pregnancy and also to be less of a burden to Monica who also had 2 jobs.

My Mother sat us down and talked to us about getting married. We actually were in agreement and proceeded to make wedding arrangements. Julian was dead set on joining the military. I begged him not to leave me. I did not like being alone and had come to depend on him so much that I felt as if I had no one else. He had a more mature way of thinking. He was a saver. I thought of my own comfort zone and getting by from day to day. He was trying to get us out of here for life.

We got married in our small church with 9 guests two days after he was sworn into the United States Army. I still remember our Pastor saying, "Do you Missy, take thee Julian, to be your lawful wedded husband.........?" I felt honored in front of our families. "And do you, Julian, take thee Missy, to be your lawfully wedded wife.........?" etc. "Ladies & Gentlemen, introducing Mr. & Mrs. Julian A. Sweetin! I only wished that my Father was there but my brother Mike proudly escorted me down the aisle.

Julian left on a Tuesday for Ft. Dix; it was very hard for me. I felt so alone and abandoned. I made all my prenatal visits and had a solid routine with work. I ate well, took Lamaze and drank a quart of milk per day. Once Julian graduated from basic training he was home in time to see the birth of our beautiful daughter, India Nicole Sweetin. She was dark like me, with thick curly hair and one dimple. It was such a joy to bring my bundle home. We were able to shop at the local PX at Ft. Dix with major discounts. I enjoyed buying things for her and picking out baby clothes.

My Mother's health was improving, but she was grieving over Daddy still, and he inexplicably did not leave a will. She offered to babysit India as a way to earn some extra money which was great because it was a hard decision to return to work. Two months passed before it kicked in that I was married with a child. After graduation from Basic Training, Julian was stationed at Fort Bragg, NC.

I read in the Trentonian that my oldest friend Evan Spencer got shot but survived. I visited him in the hospital but he had no idea who I was. I prayed for him and asked his family to keep me posted. I had planned to stay in touch, but work was crazy and unpredictable.

Like I said previously, life has a way of breaking up plans. I would frequent a luncheon establishment down the street from work for breakfast since Julian was 'AWOL' from my life. There was a cook whose back was always to me. It was something about the way he chopped potatoes and onions at the grill with two spatulas which was hypnotic. It had a rhythm and he had a rock. His shoulders were broad, and his legs were bowed. He was easily one of the best grill cooks I'd ever seen. I was impressed!

After 2 months of grilling my potatoes and onions one morning he caught me looking at him in his peripheral vision and I can see his smile from the back of his head. He put on a little show by flipping each spatula and tossing potatoes into the Styrofoam containers. When he was all done, he wiped his large hands on his stained apron and approached me. I had never seen his face before now. He was better looking from the front view! He put out his large hand to greet me as I looked up precociously from my book. It was obvious I was trying to avoid staring. It was that damn spatula rhythm, in my head, day after day. "I'm Suede" He said seductively with one eyebrow rising.

Did he have to be so damn good looking? He was charming, had light skin, dimples, strawberry colored dreads and blue eyes! His soft chest hair curled just above his unbuttoned shirt and just below his collar bone. His Adam's apple went up and down as he spoke. I put out my hand and said, "Nice to meet you, I'm Mitsy Stanley!" Fumbling, dropped the book trying to bookmark it with a napkin, spilled lukewarm coffee onto my lap, fork hit the floor and as I reached for it, bumped my head on the corner of the table! "I'm Missy Sweetin".

The left corner of his mouth went high in the air revealing the whitest teeth I'd ever seen on any man besides Jack Marshall himself! His eyes lowered and he added, "Welcome to my place Missy". I couldn't think, I said "You're welcome!" the corner of the lip went up again, but his gaze never left me. He smelled like

Halston's best and I can feel my mouth watering.

"I mean thanks, I was actually just leaving" I said thumbing toward the door but still seated. As he sat across from me, uninvited, he reached for my hand while simultaneously motioning a worker to come clean up my mess without so much as a blink. Without saying a word! My head said, 'Smooooove'. But my bottom lip dropped because I felt it. I have never seen such a thing! You beautiful thing, you! His eyelashes were curled but long, revealing those eyes, piercing and focused.

He said, "Breakfast is on me, Missy". I felt like an idiot, as he swiped a piece of potato off my chin. I was shaking and my thoughts were everywhere. I said, "I come almost every morning, I don't mind". I said, without thinking, yet thinking too fast, I said "Oh not *COME* every morning, tuh, I meant come HERE every morning, well, almost".

He leaned, what felt like 2 seconds from my face and said, "You're very beautiful you know?" I blushed, with my dark skin and dimples, I felt as if he could actually see me turn beet red! I stammered, "Uh, I really have to go, again nice to meet you Suede." I scampered out the door leaving my bag on the corner of the chair. As I returned to the door, Suede had it hanging off his index finger with 'the grin'. I thanked him and walked quickly down the street to work. 'Smoooooove!' What a man!

Although I wore my wedding ring, before I knew what happened I was spending more and more time with Suede at his luncheonette. I saved money because everything was always on the house and it was good food. After time, I would return after work to see him. He would be closing down and the door would be locked. He always had a Pepsi for me waiting, with ice.

We made love every time I visited in his back room apartment. He had lava lamps and beanbag chairs. He had a lot of Bob Marley and Carlos Santana on wax. My Mother had begun to notice that I wasn't coming straight home to get India and I was running out of lies. She knew. Anytime I came late, she would bring up Julian. I don't know if she could smell Suede on me or if she just was guessing or if she had some experiences herself. I dare not ask. But she knew. She'd sit in the rocker with India and she would mention that Julian is due to come home or that she's surprised that Julian hadn't called. Then she'd say, "Well you wouldn't have been here if he did". I would not respond.

T. E. Williams

Chapter 4 "Left Right Left"

Julian was halfway across the world in Desert Storm. That's where I put him, that's where he will stay. Why oh why did my Mother convince me we needed to get married? I didn't take my vows seriously enough. I didn't think of consequences or broken hearts. Julian was always there and Julian will always be there for me and India. It was just the circumstances, the struggle, the hunger that brought us together. That, and not using condoms.

We were exclusive, weren't we? We had to bail our Mothers out, didn't we? We needed each other in convenience, right? It didn't mean we had to sacrifice our own selfish desires to survive! Did it? He left me, I hadn't left him. I justified it in my mind. I'm only 20! He is too! He's probably shacked up with someone as we speak! Some tough Army girl from Detroit! That was my rationale…

Until he came home! I knew that I looked phony greeting him. It felt awkward. He grabbed India and bent down to kiss me. He looked good. I couldn't look him in the eye. He hugged his Mother and asked, "Hey Miss, did you get any of my letters?" Before I could speak his mother interjected, "They all came at the same time son, so I left them on the mantel for her, she hasn't seen them yet." She said with a broad smile. He then said, "Wait, you haven't been here?" I said, "Oh, well sometimes I just stay at Mom's it's just easier on gas". I felt so ashamed. Our city is 7 miles in diameter. You could get from my Mother's to his Mother's in 7 minutes! This man *knew* me. We didn't need words.

As he brought his large green duffle into our room, he must've felt me behind him because he turned suddenly and looked at me. I was scared! All the blood rushed out of my face and my lips felt instantly chapped! I must've swallowed like 3 times consecutively as I looked up at his 6 foot frame which had filled out quite a bit in training. I can see the lightening vein pop in the middle of his forehead with his caramel skin. He dropped the bag, picked me up off my feet and swept me onto the queen sized bed. He kicked the door with his boot and looked down at me. "I love you Missy". He kissed me very deeply and we made love with our clothes still on. I was really surprised because with his Mother's comment and my bloodless face, I thought he figured it out.

It was just so one-sided. Passionate on his side, robotic on my side and he seemed to take forever. As I lay on my back braless with my shirt unbuttoned, he stroked the space between my breasts with his middle finger. "Whatchu been doing Miss?" I said, "Just working hard to match what you're doing, that's all man." He said, "You look good baby." I said, "You do too." I stopped just short of saying 'Suede'. Oh, why did I get myself into this? All my reality just came back with the near slip of the tongue. I wouldn't even be able to play that off! If Suede's name was George, John, Jacob or even James, I could play it off! His name is butter in my mouth, the softest vanilla ice cream and sweet sugar daddy caramel, mmm, Suede. And I want to go lay my head on his chest and let him make me some naked ass eggs and toast. I don't want to be here remembering what *what's his name's* name is! I don't want to be in this bed. I want Suede! Dammit! It's gonna be a long night.

"Bay, how long are you home for?" He replied, "Just 3 days, I have to report to Dix on Friday." Dammit! Dammit! Friday? Suede ain't having that shit! What the fuck? We gotsta get you outta here! Think fast rabbit! "Oh well, at least we have you for a little while", I said with my teeth clenched. He said, "'Fraid not sweetie, I have to get up at 0600 to facilitate the meeting for the marksmanship of the newbies for their AIT". It honestly sounded like BLAH, BLAH, BLAH, BLAH, WHOMP, WHOMP! "Oh, I understand, well we have tonight" I said nodding. He began to snore.

By the morning, he was up and out for a run. He would want to eat upon his return so I sat on the foot of the bed fumbling with my feet for some slippers thinking, 'I don't even sleep here'. I find one slipper and drop to my knees looking for the other, locate it and stand up. Julian is standing in the doorway with the smell of bagels wafting in the air. "I was just going to make you some breakfast, hun", I said getting to my feet. He replied, "I just had a breakfast bar and some vegetable juice, I'm okay, you eat". I grab the bag and tear into the sandwich. Everything bagel, cream cheese, bacon; my favorite! With a large coffee. Julian kissed me, whispered, "I love you Missy" and darted out the door. I watched part of 'Alien Nation' then got up played with the baby as my Mother in Law fed her cream of wheat and fruit. I showered and got ready for work, kissed India and left.

As soon as I arrived to work, John poked his head in my office to let me know that we would be receiving a visit from the governor. I told him "Thanks for the warning!"

That afternoon, Christine Todd Whitman and her entourage walked through our West State Street office with the press snapping photos and flipping their note pads. Ugh!

I put on the 'Company Face' and said to myself, "Showtime!" John made sure I was available for the press conference and prepped me on what I should and should not say. It went well.

Although I had no political aspirations I could see myself in that line of work. I loved being in the spotlight and being the center of attention, even if it was to be a token for John's agenda. Upon hiring me, John once asked if I had any negativity in my background history. I immediately thought of my recent infidelity, but did not reveal it to him. I said no, but he said everybody has something. I told him I had once posed for Trentonian's Page Six, a centerfold bikini model in the local paper. He was satisfied.

Chapter 5 "Lesson Learned"

As I walked into the luncheonette I felt a stinging sensation in my eyes as Suede was pouring water on the hot grill for the morning wipe down. He did this often which caused steam to waft all over the cafe. I can see his dreads melting from the heat. They fell sweaty and flat against his cheek, which clenched right at his mandible in such a manly way when he bit down. He wiped his brow with the back of his wrist.

Then Suede began scraping one spatula against the other in that rhythmic way that caught my attention in the first place. I let the aroma pass my nose and closed my eyes breathing in his Halston and his effervescence. I held my head back to reminisce on this moment later alone. The sound of the spatulas clinging as if they were chanting 'Suede, Suede, Suede, Suede', like his own cheering section.

As he wiped his hands on his apron, I backed out the door. That was enough for me to get through the day.

When I came down for lunch, Suede stopped everything and came to my table. He looked deeply at me, "You okay Missy?" He said, to which I replied, "Oh, yeah, I want a BLT w/Mayo", his worker Ms. Evelyn had heard the order and already had the bacon out of the bin and was slicing a fresh tomato after popping down the wheat bread. He got them traint! (not trained) and people in line rolled their eyes.

Suede sat down across from me as he'd done so many times, "I missed you at breakfast" he said softly, bit his lip and tilted his head. I said, "It's my baby, she's not well". He looked at me with the corner of his lip going up and said, "Oh, you sure? Is that all? Because I thought since your husband came home you wouldn't be in at all today. I thought you'd be... entertaining, or exhausted." I felt my mouth drop. Do I got a stalker? Is Suede crazy? I replied, "Uh...oh you know huh?" He said, "Yes". Then he suddenly got up and walked over to the ringing phone.

"Suede" He said in a domineering voice. "You want toast? Turkey Bacon? Straight". Ms. Evelyn looked up from the register, "Sampson?" Suede nodded. He walked over to me again and said, "Playtime over. You're late". Losing track of time, I looked at my watch, sprang up and out the screen door.

It was incredibly difficult to focus at work. I messed up a Job Line Ad for a Legislative Analyst last week. Mindy, the hater, made sure she told me as I removed my jacket and put it on my chair. The ad read:

'Registered Animal needed for busy down town lobbying firm; 5 years experience required, transcripts reflecting public service electric and gas is desirable. $45k. Please send resume to: etc'...

I was called into John's office to discuss my focus issue. He explained that this is a very detail-oriented position and that was discussed with me during my interview. I apologized for the error and restored confidence into John who initially hired me and had backed me up continually against the nay-sayers in the office, including Mindy. I honestly think he hired me for two reasons: 1) I was his token Black, 2) He liked saying Missy n Mindy like we were gonna be friends or something. John said, "Missy, don't make a fool out of me". That was it! I offered, "Not trying to make an excuse for this horrible error, John, but my husband is fighting in Dessert Storm and I do miss him. Please allow me to retract." He understood but said from now on he would personally be proofreading before it goes to print. I understood.

PSE & G? C'mon Missy!

After work I hustled down to the luncheonette to find Suede sitting with a young lady with blonde hair and long nails; got a bad vibe, backed out the screen door. I went home, rubbed Mommy's feet, played with India and cooked salmon and rice for them. Fell asleep in Monica's bed who was working overtime. India was such a sweet baby. She curled up next to me and fell asleep in my arms.

It had been 3 weeks since I backed out of Suede's place and I was really horny. I played with the 'Magic Button' and smoked a cigarette. I jumped up got ready for work as Mommy and India were watching Barney.

As I entered the parking lot of the Firm, I got a strange vibe. Just then a familiar song came on the radio as revealing to me as the nose on my face; 'Torn between two lovers, feeling like a fool. Loving you both is breaking all the rules'. What the heck is wrong with me? I have a husband, honorable and true, busting his ass for us over in another country! Fuck Suede! I got fingers! I turned the car off, snatched the keys out and exited the car. Suede was standing in the lot!

I said, "Suede? " He said, "Missy I need to talk to you" He threw his dread back. I entertained him, "Yes Suede" as he walked closer. He said, "Missy I'm getting a divorce." I threw my hands up "You're married? I can't do this right now Suede, I have to focus on this job! You never said you were married!" Of course, such is life, Mindy pulls her cavalier into the lot. "Look Suede, I have to go I'll call you."

As I go into work John calls me into his office to show me yet another error on a Job Line Ad. I couldn't believe it! I know we both checked this ad together. He showed me the Ad I'd done. Then he showed me the finished product. He apologized to me profusely. "I don't understand John" I said. He breathed heavily and said "Mindy was caught sabotaging your campaigns; I had to let her go." Mouth......dropped! He continued, "Turns out she felt envious that you were advancing so quickly after she's been here 10 years. I am truly sorry Missy." Mindy was coming to collect her things!

Lesson learned.

Chapter 6 "The Life"

After finding out I was pregnant for the 3rd time, I decided not to have the baby. Not that it was an easy decision, but the timing could not have been worse. I booked an appointment at the local clinic, passed protesters, 6am to get it 'taken care of'. My husband had been away too long and it was a reasonable deduction to know that it was Suede's baby. I went alone. The clinician was cold, the table was cold, the utensils and apparatus were cold and my heart was cold. Life has a way of teaching but you have to get it the first time. If you don't, the lesson is bitter, and your life will be harder.

Because my mother was not well, I resigned my position at the Firm. The truth is, the place reminded me of Suede and I couldn't stomach going back there. John and his staff threw me a party and lo and behold ordered catered food from Suede's luncheonette. He personally delivered the sandwiches.

He rang the bell and I buzzed him in.

His hands were too full so I approached the door and cracked it. He said, "How are you Missy?" I said, "I'm fine Suede, how're you?" He said, "How come you never came back?" I said well you were there after hours with your lady and I didn't want to interrupt". He looked at me and replied, "That was my daughter." I winced, "Your daughter?" He scoffed, "Yes, Ariel, my daughter. I wanted you to meet her. You and I were getting pretty serious and I felt since she was going to be working with me she ought to meet you. Carol and I have been separated for 2 years. Go get John."

I went to collect the money from John with the tip and handed it to him. He turned, and walked out. I followed, "Suede, I have to tell you something." Without turning, he replied, "Already know. My Homey was there with his girl on the same morning." I dropped my face and walked away.

Saturday morning I woke up and heard the sounds of music from my East State Street 1st floor apartment. I threw on some sweats, brushed my teeth, tied a silk scarf on my head and sat on the porch. It was hot, 'round 92 and it wasn't even 10:00am. I could see the heat rise on the asphalt. My Mother In Law and India had already been up and out. They could be anywhere. She liked to shop. I gave her cash by the handful.

DJ Juice walked up and sat on the porch with me. We talked about his latest mixed tape which I had to have for the ride. I dug in my pocket and found a crumpled up $10 bill. He looked at it and popped it out, stuck it in his pocket handing me 2 tapes and dipped off.

They were already acting crazy outside down in the 'Boat Section'. All the cars had gigantic speakers booming, riding with the hatch backs open. My girlfriend Mookie hadn't seen me in a while and pulled up when she saw me. "Hey girl, I been trying to catch up to you for a while." I said, "Whassup Mook?" She and I shared a hospital room together on the maternity ward. She was discharged before me and we've been cool ever since. We both had girls. "I left my job to help Mommy and to take care of India." She said, "I got an opportunity for you since you have a car; Quick money, quick work." Sounded good at the time. She told me that Scotto and Sarge, 2 homeys from 'round the way need someone to make runs to New York every week for a package, $200 per run. Sounded lovely since my savings were dwindling and Julian's checks were few and far between. I told her I was with it. She'd let me know when they were ready.

From then on, India and I spent more time at Julian's Mother's. India was always with her. I was hitting the turnpike for that almighty dollar. Scotto and Sarge were decent. They didn't talk much but loved weed. They rolled blunt after blunt. Sometimes they would light one and roll one at the same time. They had an odd way of passing. Sarge would toss the lit blunt to Scotto and vice versa.   I started smoking weed with them, but could not roll it. Weed was alright; I could smoke and drive and still knew what was going on. I always thought weed was like acid. They said if I smoke with them I have to learn how to roll a blunt.

Every trip up the turnpike to the city was eventful with these two. They paid me well, fed me and tossed the weed. I must've made over 50 trips up the turnpike with them. We'd come back 'round Fountain and chill over Scotto's crib. His room was cool. He had tables full of blow, weed, scales and crack.

He had 2 scanners which monitored everything the cops did. We knew *who* was gonna be raided, when, and every set up coming. He would offer me $100 more just to cut the crack in small pieces with a razor and bag up the weed. I never had so much cash! And free weed. Sarge started giving me enough weed to sell on East State to the Boat Boys. It was easy. And I can pick and choose when I wanted to sell.

I could have all my time with India and Mommy until I got paged. Even when Julian called, nothing was gonna come between me and my money.

One of the Boat Boys, Power, would come over to buy weed and roll his Boat right there in my room. He always asked for a glass of milk, which I always had. He would soak the weed in the 'Boat Juice' and put a cigarette in the little vanilla bottle it came in for 'the head' (to one's self). He called it *Sherm*. I kept fans on because the smell was terrible. My Mother In Law would be at work. I couldn't imagine smoking one. After a while I got used to the smell. It was like that all year long.

He would pull up a milk crate and roll each joint of Boat, which, when turned green, he would wrap in individual foil papers. When he got to 10 individual joints, he would have what is known as a 'bundle' and I would wrap the entire 'wap' of 10 in one big foil square. He would pay me a bundle if I ripped the foil for him and give a bundle for 'The House' which meant he rolled in my house.

Power was a good dude. One time, he stashed 8 bundles near my house because Jakes were around. I found the stash after they left. He gave me $50. He was looking for it for 2 days.

Ever since I moved to East State I always kept a switchblade with me in the car. On this one occasion, I was glad I did because Sarge *tried my chin*. When we got back to Trenton from the city, he jumped out on me at the light at Calhoun & Church right in front of Klotz Bar!

He didn't think I would jump. I jumped. I caught his ass right on the bridge, my blade to his neck!

I had become a Queen Pin, Pimptress, Drug Diva. My rep was on the line and I'll be damn if I let this knuckle head run off with my dough! Did he get too comfortable? Did he think shit was sweet? The knife was at his temple now and we were the same height leaned over the bridge! I told him "Just because Scotto ain't ride today you gone try to fuck me out my cut? Hell no Nigga! Now run me my ends or I'll cut you and throw you in the fuckin' canal!"

He reached in his back pocket and gave up the knot. I moved the blade from his temple to just under his nose. I had him by the neck, broad daylight. I snipped the skin between his nostrils with the tip of my blade and as the blood ran down his white T, I held his head back and spit in his nose. "I play for keeps Motha Fucka! And I don't want to HAVE this fuckin' conversation again! Now get the fuck outta here before I kill ya damn kids!" I demanded. I got scared when he darted off because I hadn't realized I had an audience and I was not from North. Shiloh Baptist Church was just 10 feet away. I felt ashamed. I got back in my Saab, which was still running and dipped off.

Power came through that morning. He knocked on the door and as I opened it he had his fist cupped over his mouth giggling. "Yo, you a wild girl yo!" He said as he brushed pass me in my hallway holding a bagged 40 of Red Bull. He put his forearm in his stomach and bent all the way over laughing. "You crazy Miss, what the fuck you was gonna do if he had a gun?" I said, "You heard about it?" He said, "Trenton ain't THAT big!" I was trying not to smile. He told me, "Them boys got raided up on Sweets last night." I thought about it, my eyes darted back and forth. I ain't have nothing to do with that shit. He read my mind.

Power said, "Don't worry, his baby Moms was the one who called because he hit her. That crazy bitch on a rampage!" I breathed easy. He said, "You really duin this, huh?" I turned and walked into my room. I told him I was fair with Sarge. I said, "I could've killed him!" He said, "That's the life, Missy."

Power had a lot of respect for me and never did me dirty. Power was also the only person I let do dirt in my house. They say 'Don't shit where you eat'. As he pulled his hoodie off and it was still over his face. I kissed his chest. He said, "Whoa! Oh, okay, whassup Miss? Don't start shit you can't handle." My mouth gaped open and I looked helplessly up at him and licked my lips. Power took me into his arms and it was on. He was tenacious! This time, there was no tenderness, no kissing, no softness. Just pure no holds barred fucking. Power hit it from the back and I screamed in agony as he plunged in and out without regard for the sound. The more he thrusts, the more I come.

He stopped banging long enough to place his big lips and wet tongue on my open pussy and sucked from the back with recklessness! He bit my clit, R Kelly in the background.

Then he stuck his dick further. He had no mercy! Next thing I knew I was in the air. You would think I was weightless the way he switched positions and my mind said how'd I get here? Then, he was seated and bouncing me up and down on his dick. He grabbed my throat and bounced me all the way down. My tits were bouncing all over and his hand went from my throat to my left tit. I can smell his ecstasy. This man is fucking the shit outta me!

My thick black hair was bouncing hitting my right nipple, which he had so hard you could hang keys off it. My spine was on fire. He slid me off of him and put me on my knees in front of him. I sucked on him with no control. He was holding the back of my hair in a knot and when he pulled back one good time, my mouth was full. It was the best fucking I had ever had!

As he pulled me up to lie on his chest, he stroked my cheek. He said, "You know you mine now right?" I closed my eyes still throbbing, heart pounding, 'Magic Button' singing and chest heaving, I manage to spit out, "Mmmmhmm". Knowing I wanted to say 'Boy shut up I can't even squeeze my pussy Killa!' He dozed off saying, "Don't hurt me." I was thinking, 'Don't hurt YOU?!!'

Chapter 7 "New Found Power"

From that point Power was MINE. We ate, slept, and balled and bathed together. Dreams of buying houses, cars, and clothes and having little boys named Power all up in my head. Power was the *man* in the Section and I was on his arm. He had moved me up to the 3rd floor of my apartment building and we lived together for 3 whole years.

It was non-stop! Power would go outside and make $1000 then I would go outside and make $1000, in less than 30 minutes. Then we would take India and go out to eat. Power would take me on shopping sprees and buy real furs and leathers of every color for India and me. We ate the very best and I knew Power had my back. My Mother would come get India and we would hit the highway. Atlantic City, New York, anywhere I wanted to go. New Hope, PA was our little get away and we would stay for days.

Jacuzzis, massages, the freak shop and the leather stores; I loved New Hope; it was my 'Get outta the hood free' spot. Plus, it was good powder money down there.

Power had big dreams. He said, "Missy, you live for today, and not for our lifetime. We have to prepare for tomorrow, for us, for India". He was right. I was running through all kinds of cash for comfort. I paid my Mother's bills by the month. She would never be without power again in the dark, cooking on a kerosene heater. India had her name in pink lights all over her room! On East State! We had wall to wall plush carpet, heat lamps in our sit-down shower stall, his/her sinks and walk in closets. We had an arsenal under the floor and shotguns in plain view, security doors too! And nothing wasn't fucking with that.

The cost of the arsenal alone could have paid for a year of college tuition! And my jewelry! Burgundy Helzberg boxes all over my dresser! I went from gold watermelon slices on Onyx to teardrop diamond earrings with 10 matching gold and diamond rings on each finger. It's not as if I'd never heard it before. I'm not so good with saving money.

We could have bought a beautiful house in Hamilton Township and lived safely in the cut. For what Power spent in lingerie at Victoria's Secret and Chanel just to please me he could finance 2 houses, not to mention my fly ass hair salon trips and shoes from Journey. It was all for vanity. Power began to put large amounts of money away. I was too, but not as much as he was. I had so much going on but we were getting hot.

Julian pulled up in front of our apartment building and went into his Mother's place on the 1st Floor. I hadn't even talked to him in about a year. His Mother knows what I do and I never tried to keep it from her. She also knew about Power so I guessed Julian did too. I felt like, 'Dumb Fuck, you shouldn't have left me in the first place!'

That is, until he came back out with a tall thin woman in fatigues, super light skin, translucent, with a very big ass walking hand in hand with India. She looked like a potato chip. She put India into a seatbelt in the back of his car, ass all over the place! Oh HELL NO! I glared at her. Who the fuck was SHE? Stupid Missy! Did you think he was just going to stay in Dessert Storm forever? Did you think you would never see him? Your dumb ass lives upstairs from his Mother! Was he not supposed to go on with his life? Did he die in the war? You are STILL MARRIED, HELLO!

He had dressed India in some pink Garanimal type outfit, tights, and shoes I'd never seen. She looked so corny! Her hair was done in one big pony tail brushed up with a big pink bow and she wore a yellow sweater. I don't dress my baby like that! I dress her FLY! Her hair is always in beads and they always match her outfit! I pay Shanika good money! They got her looking all country! I was pissed.

I put on Tims, put some Vaseline on my face, tied my hair up and shot downstairs. Power was making a sale on the corner. I pulled fat ass Potato Chip out of the car by her weave and starting wailing on her. I'm only 4' 10! India screamed, "Maaaaaa NO!" Julian came out and pulled me off of her under my arms and my feet were still kicking. Power ran down East State pulled out his 40 Cal and shot into Julian's tire. I screamed, "No my baby is in the car!" The girl hit me with 2 good shots while Julian held me. "Get the fuck off me! Now!" I screamed! Then Power and Julian were fighting hard. You could hear each blow! Julian ain't no punk, but Power is crazy! He fights with his head!

I got India out of the car and ran in the house. From the window, sad scene, as red and blue lights swirled and sirens rang out. They had Power against the hood of the cruiser and were shaking him down. Everything he had on him was on the hood of the car. He's going down.

My lip was bleeding and a chunk was missing out of it. She got in some good shots but I was being held by Julian. I stood in the window with a paper towel to my lip. India was crying in my arms. She was 7 years old now. It was a foolish thing I did. I promised I would never let her see something like that again.

My Mother came to pick India up after the scene was over. Power and I always had a plan if one of us was going down. I had his bail money all ready by morning, only to find out there was no bail. At court on Monday morning, they called his name: Carlos Antonio Vargas, please stand! The gavel hit and it was over. Sent up to County with priors, warrants, a secret indictment, and strike 3.

I held it down, made all my visits and wrote letters to my man. I really did have love for Power. I had to take over his business. I had become the ultimate Queen Pin and had to hire 3 bodyguards who got paid well. I didn't have to lift a finger because I had runners. I always kept that heater on my thigh and the same blade in my car that cut Sarge.

I embraced the part. I had been a Teacher's Assistant and Legislative Assistant. Now I was the boss.

There were some new young thugs on my block and I had some rich White clientele to work with out in PA. I began to sell 'weight' as opposed to dipping. I sold drugs to drug dealers. I had excellent connections in place. Never dirty.

As I entered the door from a White Run, I got my mail out of the box placing my sunglasses on top of my head. I received an invitation to a family reunion for the Marshalls, my Father's side, and a package addressed to Power which read 'Cruise Tickets Do Not Bend'. I was actually debating if I should go to the reunion. I also received a letter from Mercer County Courthouse which I tore open with my teeth leaving red lipstick on the envelope.

Julian had filed for divorce and asked for full custody of India. I knew it was coming. Bastard! I had actually thought that it was news about Power. What happened? Life was going by way too fast. What had I learned? What lesson was there for me in this? I stuck my mail into my Gucci bag and walked into the apartment up the stairs. Lost in thought, I dropped my keys by the door.

As I bent down to pick it up I heard a 'click'. "Leave 'em down there and step back bitch!" Damn! Now what? I stammered, "Whatchu want man? I don't keep nothing here!" Just then, my large Crizal sunglasses fell from off the top of my head which startled him and he shot my door just over my shoulder. His next shot jammed. "Fuckin' Amateur!" I reached under my skirt to my strap got my 38, cocked it and lit his chest up! He dropped his gun. I pulled again and I got him in the thigh. Three of my guys were still at the door downstairs and I couldn't hear them running up after my shots were fired, just a high pitched whiz. Two kicked the shit out of him; the third got me out of there. They were all vested, ready, careful. This fool couldn't have been alone; he ain't that stupid.

It was too hot. Power's boys moved me and India out to Hamilton the next day. It was a new young thug, thought he could fuck with the Queen. Missy don't bother no fucking body! I just make my fucking money and leave niggas alone. That was enough for me. We can all eat! These selfish-ass new young ass thugs!

My Mother came over to get India. It was too much and I had some decisions to make. My Mother kissed me and said, "Where did I go wrong? This is not what I had in mind for you Missy. What kind of life do you want for India? Don't you want to have a family? Have more children? You disposed of a perfectly good man!" I said, "Don't worry Mommy you ain't gonna have to bail ME out!" She took India's hand and walked down the stoop and stopped.

She said without turning, "Yeah, baby, I know. But am I gonna have to bury you? Am I gonna have to BURY you?" I really looked at my Mother as she was descending. She was still so beautiful. She was tired of it; tired of me; just tired. She didn't deserve it and yet, I was still *her* baby girl.

T. E. Williams

Chapter 8 "Family Reunion"

I woke up looking like a raccoon because I hadn't taken my make up off the night before. I was up all night writing Power. I got his letter yesterday and I promised I would reply as soon as I received it. Power was actually quite the writer. His letters were filled with compliments and regrets. He didn't blame me for his incarceration. He said he wanted to propose to me and was beginning to think of our future. He had planned a trip to Cancun for us. Mookie's name popped up on the caller ID and I just let it ring. I just didn't have time.

Why is it every time a man is thinking of my future, I blow it? I was still a good looking woman, great body, still smart, I said to myself in front of my mirrored closet bouncing my leg on one toe admiring myself. Then I reached for my own throat thinking. I could not stomach the thought of dealing with any more men;

getting to know him, having him meet India, admitting what I do for a living; I am done. And I meant it.

I got out of my own head and began to get ready for the family reunion which was going to be held at the West Trenton Ballroom at 2pm. I mulled over what to wear standing at the closet. I pulled my hair back, kept my forearm across the top of my head pointing my ducky lips to the left, clicking my teeth.

I decided on my one piece royal blue pant outfit and blue heels. It was stylish, cool and if they want to play horse shoes I can always throw on my Jordans. I took a shower, got dressed, put on my makeup and tossed a large brimmed white hat on my head and threw my Jordans in a huge white bag.

My Mother had India still and they were to meet me at the Ballroom. I jumped on #29. I got to the reunion in record time, fashionably late to make an entrance. The hall was decorated in the same blue I was wearing. They had a table with blue T-Shirts with white lettering which read, 'Marshall Family Reunion' and 'WE are Marshall'. As people came to introduce themselves, I spotted Michelle and Margie fanning themselves with programs. "That's Jack's baby girl there, looking like her Mama" one Marshall said, and, "She shaped just like Donna", another said. And there's always that *one*, "Ms. 5000! Her Mama thought she was all that too." 'No', I thought, 'My Daddy ain't want your ass so you settled for his cousin!'

I excused myself and shot over to the table where my sisters were seated. "Where's India?" said Margie looking exaggeratedly behind me. They both hugged me and Michelle looked into my eyes and said, "How you duin, Miss?" I told her I was fine, but I could never lie to Michelle. She saw it. "India's coming with Mom." I replied to Margie without breaking our gaze. Michelle mouthed, "I gotta go pee."

Michelle always knew subliminally just how to accommodate. I shot behind her "Me too!" We get to the nicely decorated and pretty smelling bathroom and she looked at me in the mirror. She said, "How's Power?" sounding so sincere. I replied, "It's over Chelle, there's no bail and I'm just trying to get through it." She hugged me and rubbed my back. She was still so frail, my string bean, and I felt like I was going to break her when she hugged me.

We made our way back to the table. Margie had ordered us a round of Cosmos and I sipped it slowly with my eyes closed. Margie was already 3 Cosmos ahead of us. She was quiet and leaning, not like her at all. Mark and Mike came in the door both smartly dressed in suits of similar color with their wives at the same exact time. They shook hands, kissed each other's mates and made their way over.

"Where's Mommy?" Mark asked as I stood to hug both of them and said, "She'll be along, she's got India; probably trying to tackle that hair!" We all giggled and my pager went off. Not today. I ain't working today. As I glanced at it quickly I saw that it was Mookie again. I said to myself wow Mookie a lonely bitch today. I put the pager back into my purse.

Margie grabbed my arm as if suddenly waking up and shouted, "Oh girl they called our table!" All of us were up out of our seats and in line; Ladies before the gentlemen, of course. I kept looking at the door to see if Mommy and India were coming in. It was about an hour and 35 minutes into the reunion; not like her. I grabbed some plates and passed them down, plastic utensils, and a napkin. The spread was really nice, they had Swedish meatballs, wings, rolls, sliced ham, an assortment of salads, mac n cheese and 3 whole pans of greens and green beans. Monica and Patrick came in. Patrick had gotten to be a little man! He looked a lot like his Father and I hugged them both tightly.

I hadn't noticed it upon entrance, but there was a big painted portrait of our Father on an easel along with other members of the Marshall clan who died on their own easels. Mark touched me softly and tilted his head in the direction of the beautiful portrait. I beamed with pride.

Mike said, "After this we all are going out to Moody Park to play some games. Yeeeeaaah!" Mark said, "All these years went by and we haven't been to Moody Park together, I miss you guys." All the sisters said, "Aww" in unison and Mark blushed. My brothers were so good looking. They were with good women.

Margie was married briefly. She married a Jamaican guy and then killed him with a Phillip's head screwdriver in her Cadillac. Crazy girl defended herself and actually got off on self-defense. Her bail was set at $250,000 no 10%. There was a rumor she threatened the judge. Only Margie! She only did 3 weeks in jail! Margie, like my Father became an Auto Mechanic. But she truly was a Jackie-of-all-trades just like him. I could never tell Margie someone shot at me or she'd be right back in jail.

Michelle was still waiting for the perfect mate and we all secretly felt she was waiting for 'The return of Daddy.' She was always Daddy's girl anyway. She had her own business and had put everything into it. She was such a successful person. I was really proud of her. I'd followed in her footsteps for so long I hadn't even realized when she became so strong. She looks a lot like Mommy though, especially her hands.

Monica had gone back to school and earned her Master's in Social Work and Patrick was her main focus. She was such a lovely woman and looked a lot like Mommy too. She was always for all of us, always in our corner keeping us together. She was the best big sister on the planet and she never judged me.

As the line proceeded, I did a time check. 4:00p.m. I wanted to check the parking lot, at least, but I'm not getting out of line now. I've started dishing and grabbed a bottle of water and headed back to the table, pausing for Margie. We finally sat giggling about the spread and exchanged pleasantries.

Just then the emcee got on the microphone and tapped it once.

"Unfortunately we have to cancel these evening's festivities. You will be notified of any further changes upon clarification or more news."

We all looked in bewilderment at each other and heard gasps around the hall. The emcee motioned with the mike for Mike to come up and they pulled him in a private back room. We were whispering, "What'd they call Mike up for?" Mark went right behind him clearing his throat and stating in an authoritative tone, "I'll get to the bottom of this...excuse me." He rose and left. We slanted toward him in our seats confused.

We heard Mike scream with panic, "No! No! Lord Jesus, No!" Mark came running back to the table! I froze. I knew.

He was in tears, shaking his head slowly. He pulled us all together in a huddle. "It's Mommy and India, Missy, girls, they were rushed to the emergency room but they didn't make it! They were T-Boned by the River Line at Lalor and had to be extricated from her car! India was flown to Cooper, but........Man! Mookie's been trying to call you for the past hour!"

I screamed then collapsed. We were all inconsolable. My child is dead! My dear Mother is dead! They're dead! I couldn't stop crying. It was not possible! "Lord Jesus, please! Help me!" I shouted. "This cannot be!" I cried and rocked! Michelle and Margie were on their knees crying and Mike had come back from the private room yanking on his tie, tears in his eyes. He is our parents' first born. He was the patriarch now, after Father died. Monica cried and prayed and prayed and cried, and cried and paced. Marshalls were coming over to our table after hearing the news crying and saying, "I'm so sorry!" and "What a tragedy!" It was all so unreal! They yelled, "And the baby! Lord Why?" My child and my Mother are dead. I could not breathe. Flashbacks of her in my arms at her birth began to invade me, the sound of her cry, and I saw her walking toward me; her first steps with my arms outstretched; her handing me the picture she was so proud of; her seated between my legs as I made her pony tails; her standing in her brownie uniform and finally, her walking hand in hand with Potato Chip. My angel is gone. "No! not my India!!" I screamed! "Not my only *living* child!" My tears ran down and I buried my face into my hands as I flashed back to my beautiful Mother lifting her head to kiss my Father; everything moving fast through India's flashback, yet very slow motion in my Mother's. I gave it up softly through my wet lips, "Mommy!!!!"

The Marshall family surrounded us, "Step back! Give her air!" We all huddled together after they helped me off the floor. I looked at the faces of my sisters and brothers and again passed out with grief. A nameless Marshall hustled us to a car and drove us to my house.

I do not remember the ride, but I remember laying my head on some big breasted lady. She was rocking me.

Next thing I knew I was in my bed. I jumped up! "I want to see my Mother!" I screamed! "I want to see my baby!" My guard came in trying to hold me and I smacked him in the face and punched him in the chest over and over with my fists, screaming. Another man barged in; he looked like my Father. He handed me a pill and tilted a glass of water toward me and said, "Daughter, trust me." I rocked back and forth, looked toward the ceiling taking the pill, swallowing the water. I fell backward on the bed then drifted off to sleep.

Later I found out that the Marshall man who barged in was Reverend Marshall, a family member on my Father's side I'd never met. He was my Father's Uncle from Hopewell. As I drifted off, the large breasted woman sat next to me on my bed, grabbed my limp hand and began to pray as I surrendered.

"Father God, maker of Heaven and Earth, you are the Alpha and Omega, the beginning and the end. You are the creator and finisher of our Faith.

Lord I do not know what plans you have for the life this woman, I do not know, Lord, what her journey has been, nor do I know what her life will be like after this day, but Lord, Father God, this is your child, created in your image, and she needs the great and mighty comfort of your hand on her heart. Take her into your bosom. Show her that you are who you promised in the Bible. She needs you Lord, I trust you Lord, this family needs you. Give her a new light as only you can. In the mighty name of Jesus. Amen."

I sat in my house naked in the dark for 2 days. I didn't answer the phone or the door. My guards wouldn't let anyone in. I was a mess. I rolled over and cried for an indeterminable amount of time. I hated myself. I got up out of the bed and sat in my oversize green corner chair with my knees to my chest crying. I wanted to hold India. I wanted to hold her. I had brought life into this world and was brought into the world by a life. Why was I still here? I wanted to die. I wanted to be with them.

A knock came to the door. I didn't want to be bothered by anyone. I was still numb. I felt completely hopeless. The knock came again, and then I heard keys. My guard had let in Margie and Michelle with Mookie right behind them. They each hugged me. Mookie hugged me especially long. She looked at me with solemn eyes, "Missy I tried so hard to reach you. It was me who called the hall once I found out where you'd gone. I am so, so sorry." I began to rock to and fro. Margie opened the mini blinds then both my sisters excused themselves to my adjacent sitting room. They sensed Mookie had something private to tell me. My sisters were always intuitive. We were such a close knit family. I miss them. I miss us.

Mookie came close to me and leaned over toward me. She wiped a tear from my eye. Then she opened her mouth slightly and held it before she spoke. "I saw the accident." She said as she put her hand on my shoulder. "I was sitting at the light on #129 parallel to the River Line in the left turning lane." She said Mommy had attempted to make a right onto #129 and her car was positioned after the barrier near the tracks.

She couldn't back up due to the barrier, yet could not go forward because of the North

Bound train to the left which was moving slowly. She looked to the left, but not the right, and the South Bound train is what T-Boned her. She said she saw that it was Mommy and said to herself, 'Lord, Ms. Donna done stopped after the barrier came down!' But Mommy should have remained. As her car proceeded there was no way to warn her.

Mookie said, "I was blowing the hell out of my horn because from where I was, the South Bound train was barreling down the tracks which she could not see." Mommy must've thought that someone was blowing *behind* her to get going. Mookie said she wishes she never blew. She felt like she was the reason Mommy continued to proceed over the tracks.

"Missy I know how much your Mother loved birds. I must tell you, and I hadn't thought of it then, but there was a red bird that came down as the train was pushing your Mother's car sideways down the track. It landed directly on the hood of my car! It looked at me kind of funny, nodded, and flew off!"

Then she added, "I left my car and ran to the payphone to call you!" I looked at her and began to cry softly. There was a 3 minute pause as she consoled me. Then Mookie said, "The red bird came to see me again, Missy" She said, "It was the same bird." I tilted my head up toward her. I looked at her strange, thinking, what the hell? Mookie has never been spiritual or claimed to be some kind of mystic. Mookie ain't even deep!

"Thank you Mook." She got up and went to the kitchen. I heard water running. She had begun to get the house together when my sisters returned to me. Margie said, "Look Miss, we got some business to take care of. We have to bury Mommy and lay India Nicole to rest. We have to go on. You got to shake this shit off." Margie was so damn tough. I just don't know how she can *go on*.

Michelle just kept rubbing my back with that bony hand barely touching me. It was annoying more than anything. She had Mommy's hands. Margie said with force, grimacing, "Missy get up and get dressed! We got work to do!"

My guard came to the door and motioned for my sisters. Monica was standing in the living room. Monica led my sisters to me and they all stood 'round me. They clasped hands when

Monica began to pray for comfort. She touched each of us with oil on our foreheads. She ended, "In Jesus' name, Amen."

They got me up and showered. They dressed me and we went down to the funeral parlor in one vehicle. Julian was already there with Potato Chip. He walked over and hugged me. I wasn't surprised. I was the one who'd become a thug, not him. His Mother was holding a white handkerchief dabbing her eye.

I threw up right there in the waiting room of Hughes. Then everything went dark. When I came to, Monica was holding me and had a cool washcloth on my forehead. She said "Julian and the military are taking care of all the arrangements. Missy, you need help." My eyes rolled back into my forehead, her voice sounded far away and I faded in and out of consciousness.

T. E. Williams

Chapter 9 "When It All Falls Down"

I woke up in a cold room and everything was crisp & white. I can hear elevators and machines beeping and also a woman's voice over a PA system calling for Dr. Phillips and Dr. Gupta. I was in a hospital. Only, why are my wrists strapped? I couldn't understand why my head had limited movement. It was also strapped! I lie for a long time wondering what was happening.

People were zooming by quickly just outside the door but wouldn't come in this room, where I am. I said, "Hello?" No one answered. Again I said, "Hello?" An officer came in and said, "Oh, Ms. Sweetin, I'll get the nurse."

A nurse and a doctor came in standing at the foot of my bed with my chart. The doctor said to me, "Yes, Ms. Sweetin, welcome to Trenton Psychiatric Hospital, I am Dr. Gupta. Although you are not here voluntarily, you will have the freedom to go about on this floor of the wing. This is your nurse, Kerry. If you need anything at all or need to use the bathroom she is here to assist you. Do you have any questions?"

Of course I had questions. "What's happening, I don't understand!" Who, who are you? Where Am I?" Dr. Gupta adjusted his position and he and Kerry looked at one another. He put his hand on his hip, cleared his throat and said, "Ms. Sweetin, you are at Trenton Psych. You were brought here by your husband who had you committed to our care. Do you understand?" I tried to sit up and I kept looking at my wrists.

"Why am I restrained? I cannot sit up!" He looked at my chart and said, "Yes, we thought that this may be best because when you were committed you fought the guards and broke another nurse's nose. After your husband explained the circumstances, they decided not to charge with a crime." He confidently pushed his glasses onto the bridge of his nose.

I smiled, "Dr. Whoeverthefuckyouare, I have been separated from my so-called husband for over 3 years and I am a grown ass woman so get me the fuck outta here please! NOW!" The doctor said with absolutely no empathy, "I'm afraid that's not possible Ms. Sweetin, you're here to get better. You are a danger and a threat to yourself as well as others. Your family has placed you with us for an indeterminable amount of time to ensure your best interest and the interest of the public." I replied, "I'm no fool. In New Jersey you have to have 2 family members and a judge to commit someone."

The nurse, interjected, "I'm afraid your sister, I think her name's Michelle Marshall has also signed the commitment papers. You've suffered a mental breakdown." I couldn't understand the words that were coming out of Kerry's mouth. Ultimate betrayal! Ultimate betrayal! "That can't be!" I rejected the news, mind, body and soul! I could not conceive of it! I screamed crying loudly, thrashing my body back and forth on the bed, but the restraints allowed me only so much movement. I kicked and screamed but they both turned and walked out.

Kerry came back with a syringe behind her back. I quickly said, "What the fuck is that?" Orderlies walked in, one Black and one White and held me down as Kerry stuck me in my arm with the injection. I soon surrendered due to the shot. The last thing I felt was my own spit and tears running down my chin and couldn't even wipe it with my own hand as the White guy said, "She'll get used to that! She's a fighter!"

I woke up as a Dietary Aide put a tray in front of me. The White orderly came in. He looked at me and said, "Ms. Sweetin, I'm Boris. I'm going to unstrap you so that you can have your lunch. Please don't make this difficult." He began to unstrap my head and wrist binds, but left my feet strapped. I sat up and rubbed my eyes. "How much time has passed? What is today, Boris?" He said, "You've been here for 3 days, you need to eat. I'll return when you're done; sorry, no utensils."

I stared down at the Salisbury steak, mashed potatoes and carrots. There was a side of tapioca pudding. "Boris, did my family lay my daughter to rest?" Boris said, "I'm sorry Ms. Sweetin, they don't tell us stuff." I looked up at him, "Call me Missy."

Kerry came in and released me to use the bathroom and take a shower. I let the warm water run all over me, soaped up scrubbed my neck and began to cry again. I toweled off and wrapped the towel around me and exited the shower. There was no mirror. I wondered what I looked like. There was a metal towel dispenser I caught a faded reflection in.

When I came back out, there was a Puerto Rican girl in the next bed. She was sucking her thumb and twirling her hair. She talked really fast and jumped from subject to subject. "Hi I'm Roxanne, R O X A N N E! I've been here for 456 days! That's over a year! Why you so dark? You want your pudding? What's your name? Your parents must be dark. You pretty. I like the pudding cuz I'm allergic to the pears but I like the pears, they just don't like me, huhuhuhuhu!" She had said it all at once and while still sucking her thumb and twirling that strand!

Kerry came back in and moved my tray table. She put a white gown on me and strapped me in. She let me know how to push the button for service and introduced me to Roxanne Cuenca, my new roommate. Roxanne said, "huhuhuhuhu we already met you late Ms. Kerry!" Kerry ignored her tucking my feet back under the covers. I asked, "Kerry, did I really have a nervous breakdown?" Kerry said, "Ms. Sweetin", I cut her off, "Missy, please." She said, "Missy, it's all confidential and Dr. Gupta will be seeing you soon. Roxanne smiled with the thumb loosely in her mouth, "Roxanne Maria Cuenca, please! Huhuhuhu!"

As Kerry left, I tried to turn my back to Roxanne. I took the time to say, "Lord, please send me a sign that my baby is with you." I dozed off having eaten half of the Salisbury steak and a bite of the carrot. Roxanne started talking, but she wasn't talking to me. Last thing I said was, 'I don't belong here' with Roxanne singing "You are my sunshine, my only sunshine, you make me happy, when skies are gray......"

It was day 6 of my involuntary incarceration and Boris came in with the big Black guy. I hadn't met him and Boris was unstrapping me for my meal. I said, "Who are you?" He put his fat sausage fingers across his chest and said, "Me? Oh I'm Travis how you doing?" I looked back and forth between the two and said, "Are you serious? Boris? And Travis? Y'all sound like cartoons!" He said, "Yeah, uh, nice to meet you Missy. They tell me you lost somebody. This world, man, say no say no." I looked at him and said, "Travis, what did you just say?" He said, "You know, say no say no." I said, "Travis, the saying is same old same old!" I can tell I was going to like him. I need some entertainment around here!

Kerry came in to tell me that Dr. Gupta will be meeting me tomorrow at 11a.m. She said that after 7 days, patients have to have an official Psycho-Social Evaluation. I calmed myself and prepared for it. I need to get out of here. Roxanne invited me on a tour of our floor taking me directly to the Common Room where there were many books, puzzles and a television. The residents were watching Highlander and I dozed, awoke and Travis took me back to my room and strapped me in with no words between us.

As Boris came to take me to my visit with Dr. Gupta in the morning, he lifted the lid on my breakfast and said, "You ain't gone eat this

Missy?" Already eating a bite of turkey sausage from the hot steaming plate, I said, "Not now Boris." He walked me down to a large locked office with awards all over. Dr. Gupta came from a private bathroom stopping Boris from strapping me to the black leather bound perforated chair in front of his large desk. "That's not necessary Boris, I can handle it." I looked at him; cocky sun of a bitch, but I held my tongue because he was my ticket out of here. As Boris left, he shut the door and I heard the keys. I directed my full attention to Dr. Gupta.

He began with, "Ms. Sweetin I understand you haven't been eating. Is the food not good?" I thought it was important to make eye contact. I also realized that he wanted to see if I can have a normal conversation, Psych 101. I smiled, "Food's fine Doc" I said, as I stood and reached over and got a peppermint out of his dish.

I unwrapped it and stuffed it in my cheek and tossed the wrapper onto his desk. "Is my Mother and my baby girl buried?" he replied, "Ms. Sweetin, we are not here to discuss that matter, however, I am here to evaluate your condition. You are a visitor with us for 45 days. If after 45 days you have demonstrated that you can rejoin society as a well productive member you may leave. Until then, you may want to be a little less attitudinal."

I nodded, "Proceed please, and call me Missy." He began with a basic spelling test and asked me the meaning of certain words. He then showed me a series of photos and I had to describe what I saw in them. We played word association, and he asked me how certain subjects made me feel; war, racism, crime, abortion, capital punishment and suicide.

I believed I had given him an honest, unbiased encapsulation of my feelings. He threw me for a loop with the last subject: Masturbation. I felt as if he was trying to trip me up. I had recently read an article which examined the link between sex and violence. I said, "What about it?" I said stoically "Well" he continued, "How do you feel about sex?" My response was, "I think that two people who love each other are entitled to express their feelings through acts of love, such as love making. But it's not the above all, be all of marriage."

I then took some written tests and Travis brought me back to my room and the straps. Roxanne rocked back and forth with the thumb to the side and said, "How you do?" I giggled, "I did okay." She said, "Your baby really dead? I'm sorry. I ain't got no kids, but if I did and that happened to me I be looking like you too. You want your lunch its lasagna ain't got no meat though." I laughed at Roxanne. "It's hard to keep up with you Roxanne!" She laughed too, "I think that's why I'm here because my brain work too fast for people. You know why I'm here?" I said, "No, Roxanne why are you here?"

Dr. Gupta probably has a whole case study on this one. She said, "I'm a Math genius like that man in Beautiful Mind. Then one day it was just too many symbols and I started seeing them everywhere." I said, "Really?" Examining her thumb she said, "Huhuhuhuhu yeah, they started talking to me!" I told her, "I hate Math. I'm more of an English girl." She looked at the window which was on her side of the room and whispered, "Blasphemy!" I actually needed to talk to somebody a regular somebody and not someone with a lot of letters behind their name. I didn't want to be analyzed.

Roxanne was still talking to the 'equal sign' when I said, "India Nicole was hit by a train in the car with my Mother. They both died." She stopped rocking, "That's fucked up the driver must have been drunk that's why I don't drive people be drunk, drunk people need to stop driving was they drunk?" Whew! This one! "I don't know Roxanne, I'm still in here. Nobody will tell me anything. They say I had a nervous breakdown."

Roxanne said, "You seem pretty normal to me! Can I braid your hair?" Having my hair touched was like a form of therapy and I needed human contact. Boris and Travis can never know that. "I said, sure why not." I rang for Kerry and she brought a comb and brush and unstrapped me. We had to sign for the comb and brush. Then she sent for Travis to take us down to the Common Room. We watched Martin and I lay my head on her lap. She started singing, "You are my sunshine, my only sunshine......." I dozed off. Travis came in complimented my hair and Roxanne's skills and took us back to our room.

Chapter 10 "Red Robin"

It was finally visiting day at Trenton Psych! Day-35 and 10 more days to go. Kerry told me one of my sisters was waiting to see me. I felt hope. I didn't care which one it was I was just happy I had a visitor. I had on white scrubs and blue hospital socks. Boris came down to unstrap me and took me to the elevator to another floor in a room with tables. He strapped me to a chair and told me that visits are monitored and pointed to a woman at a desk in a uniform and the cameras. He said, "Missy, be careful in here okay?" I thanked him and anxiously awaited the visit.

I heard the door unlock as I sat on the edge of the seat, eyes wide open. A thin woman walked in with stilettos and a black sable fur coat. On further inspection I saw that it was *my* long black sable fur coat and she had my gold diamond rings on too! It was Potato Chip! She sat and smiled pursing her thin lips and crossed her legs. I was confused. I couldn't speak!

"Hello Missy, I'm Kelli. The Army had a wonderful ceremony for India and Donna. They were buried side by side at Ewing Cemetery. They purchased lovely headstones too. I'm here to tell you that it's all over. I have your man, your house and all your money. Why on Earth would you ever leave $10,000 in a safe with India's birth date as the combination? Maybe you'll think twice before you betray such a good man!

Crazy is not the description I would use to describe my reaction! I dove to reach for her throat breaking the strap of my right hand and grabbed her by her blouse! "You BITCH! You will die today motha fucker! I'm gonna kill you! You fuckin' bitch!" I became this incredible thing with uncommon strength stood and swung the chair at her striking her! "I hate you! You gonna die motha fucker! I'm gonna make you bleed real slow when I get the fuck outta here, motha fucker!"

Boris, Travis and two other guys came running in to subdue me. I ended up on the floor squirming. Nobody was able to contain me! A male nurse rushed in and shot me with a syringe and they put a straight jacket on. Then I heard Potato Chip say, "Looks like my sister is not quite ready for release. Bye Missy."

They took me to a room with equipment I'd never seen. They put cotton rolls in my mouth and a metal stick. They put a cotton and metal clamp on my temples and shocked me repeatedly. After that I was in isolation. The room had foam rubber perforations on the walls, floor, even the ceiling. Boris sat me down hard and yanked at the straight jacket. "Damn Missy I warned you!" He walked out and the lights slammed off as he shut the door.

After two weeks, Dr. Gupta evaluated me and allowed me to return to my room. Roxanne was sleeping. I looked out the window to see June's greenery. My thoughts went back to my childhood at the gully with Mommy. I woke up feeling hungry and sore. I lay looking out of the caged window as a beautiful red robin lit down on the window sill. It was Mommy's robin! I saw it as the sign I asked the Lord for in prayer which meant they were with the Lord. 2 months went by before I accepted another visitor. Mike and Mark had come, Mookie came and all of my sisters together. I couldn't see them.

September had arrived. Kerry introduced me and Roxanne to the new physical activities director, Jowana. The Common Room was emptied and the furniture had been replaced with mats. She taught us Ti Chi, yoga and meditation. She was a nice lady and the meditation helped me with grieving. Jowana came every Monday. She treated us well. Her voice was very calming as she talked to us releasing so much stress and tension. I wish I had been meditating throughout my life like I used to with Mom and Mary. It took away the bitterness and despair I often felt. The loneliness was filled by talking to Travis and listening to Roxanne's run-on sentences.

Finally I accepted Mookie's visit. She came in and hugged me though I couldn't hug her back. She sat down and smiled. She had kind of a glow. I said, "Mookie, the red bird came!" She said, "I'm glad Sis. I want to share something with you. I think your Mom wanted me to encourage you in this time. I have come to accept the teachings of Jesus Christ. I am saved now, a new creature, Born Again. I felt a lot of guilt by introducing you to the Life. I heard about Julian's recent actions and I've prayed for him. There was a time I would have put a hit on him. Listen to me now. The Lord wants me to read the 27th Psalm to you and also let you know how you can be saved. I am not the same. If He did it for me, He can do it for you too. Will you receive Him today?"

I looked at Mookie, a little confused but happy for her. She did look different and at peace. I remember Mookie would boost our baby clothes and drink Mad Dog 20/20! Monet used to call me when Mookie passed out drunk.

"I am happy you changed your life Mook, but you are free, I'm in here. I have gone through so much...I trust you." I said. She placed her palm on my head and began to pray.

"Thank you Jesus for Missy and our friendship. She has a good heart and loves you. Jesus, you came so that we can have everlasting life. Give her the strength and opportunity to make herself

a witness of your love. Thank you Lord for what you are about to do so that she can live for you and for the uplifting of your Kingdom, In Jesus' name, Amen."

"Amen." Mookie smiled at me and said, "Missy do you believe in your heart that Jesus died on the cross for the remission of our sins, rose on the 3rd day, and is sitting with us right now?"

I said, "I do" She said you must say it. I complied with tears, "Jesus, I accept you as my Savior, and I believe you died on the Cross to save my soul. I am a sinner and you are the only one that can save me because I am a mess. I surrender to you, Jesus. Please come into my life and make me a pillar and example of your love. I believe you are alive today." Mookie hugged me and was genuinely happy for me. "Missy the Lord is going to open so many doors for you which cannot be closed. Father, don't let her be the same. Show her the difference."

"Devil mad now girl, your name is written in the Book of Life! Keep praying, it works to fight him off. He has no power over you. Missy, it is important that when you wrong someone, even think with your flesh, you must repent daily.

And always remember, there is nothing you can do to *earn* grace. You just keep the faith and His grace covers you." I looked at her and said, "What about the Ten Commandments, and eye for an eye, and sacrificing lambs?" She said, "Jesus IS the lamb. I love you and I'm happy that I completed my assignment." I said, "Assignment?" She said, "Red Robin, Miss." She read Psalm 27 and I really listened to it. I felt so relieved and comforted. He will fight all my battles for me? I just have to praise Him, be thankful, and repent. "Oh and by the way, I'm married! To a Deacon! His name is Evan Spencer. I'm Brenda Spencer now!" She said, holding up her left hand. I told her that he is my childhood friend and I congratulated her. She said, "Thank you, I know! I know *everything*!"

T. E. Williams

Chapter 11 "My Testimony"

Dr. Gupta finally signed my release which stated I was 'of sound mind' and sent it to Judge Ford. I was released on December 24th, Christmas Eve. He had given me a prescription of Prozac but I knew that I no longer needed anything but Jesus. He was my 'Rock and my Salvation'! I said my goodbyes to Roxanne, Travis, Boris and Kerry. I left a card for Jowana.

Monica came for me and took me to her home. All my siblings came to see me and were tip-toeing around. I told them I was saved, a child of the Father, a new creature. Her house was decorated beautifully. She had a massive spread, all the traditional fixings. She handed me an obituary and asked if it was going to upset me. It did, a little, but overall I knew what she was trying to do.

Christmas morning was nice. I spent the whole day playing PlayStation with Patrick and eating leftovers. Paul bought Monica a beautiful new Mercedes and took us for a ride in it. As we were riding, I remembered Mookie's words, 'Her Assignment'. When we returned, I went in a quiet corner to pray and after thanking Him, asked the Lord for *my* assignment.

On New Year's Eve I went to a church within walking distance where they were having overnight services. I just wanted to praise the Lord for all He'd done to bring me out of bondage. He is so good to me. I just want to stop everyone I see and just tell them the good news! It was a quaint little church with a woman pastor.

After service, I was eyeballing the bulletin board for some part time work when the pastor came over and introduced herself as Pastor Lina Carroll, "Did you like the sermon?" she asked. I said, "Oh, very much thank you!" She saw me looking at the bulletin board and said to me, "There's always work to do in God's Kingdom. How can the Lord use you this year?"

I said, "My name is Missy, I'm staying down the road. I'm really not sure what my *Assignment* is yet." Pastor Carroll looked at me curiously, "Your face is not revealing what it is you've gone through, but I see you've had a stumbling block." I thought to myself, 'understatement'. "I am very young in Christ and I want to bring more women like me to the altar."

Pastor Carroll pulled out her card and opened my hand. She said, "Call me, daughter. I would love to hear your testimony someday." I felt awkward about it. Where would I even start?

After that I went back to that church at least 3 times per week and Pastor Carroll and I were getting to know one another. The Lord will put people in your life once you accept Jesus. It's like a network of helping hands working together for the good of the Lord. It's how you feel when he creates in you a clean heart. You just want to share your talents, yourself, your love with everyone. No more bashing each other or tearing each other down. No hood mentality with the 'I gotsta get mine' attitude. I want to save someone from what I'd gone through; change the minds of some of these young girls who think all they have to offer is sex; fix what's broken in our community. Although I had a great childhood, I still managed to find trouble. I want to catch them before they fall through the cracks like Mama was trying to do for us in the Legionnaires. I would be dead if it weren't for the grace of God.

One day I was sitting reading the newspaper and who should I see on the front page in cuffs! Ms. Kelli Porter (Potato Chip!) She was convicted of bigamy, grand larceny, fraud and embezzlement for duping two local married men out of their savings, Julian being one of them, and for tampering with Army funds. I prayed for her. I honestly thought to myself, 'He favored me to see this. I don't usually read the newspaper.' I love how He *reveals* things to me.

On a cold Wednesday evening I ventured out all bundled up to go to the church to pray. As I ended my prayer I got off my knees and who should be standing in the pew behind me in a dashing suit and a red tie but Travis! I said, "Travis?" He looked up from praying and said, "Missy?" We hugged over the partition. He said, "You come here? Aw it's good to see you Missy."

I smiled at him, "Good to see you too Travis." Just then Pastor Carroll came down the aisle passing out hymnals. She said, "Travis you know this young woman?" I looked at Pastor and said, "Yes Pastor we're old friends." Travis said, "Missy, Pastor Carroll is my big sister!" I was really surprised I hadn't seen the family resemblance. I always felt the attraction between Travis and me, but I didn't want to fall in the pattern I relied on all my life. I read in the Bible that a man chooses a wife. Before I knew it, Travis and I were spending every day together. Travis Carroll had 3 sisters, all saved. They were originally from North Carolina. Good people. Lina held the family together after their parents passed.

I went to court and answered the divorce uncontested. We didn't own any property together; Potato Chip stole my house and money. What I lost, the Bible promises I'll get back, if not here then in my Heavenly home. I don't need to store up treasures on Earth. Travis feels the same.

Travis asked to marry me on the very day my divorce became final, March 7th! It was quite liberating to look him in the eye and say, "I'm afraid not Travis, I need some 'Missy time' first!

The good Lord will let me know when I am ready to have a husband for the right reason in the right season. I trust Him 100%!

Travis and I are different than any relationship I have ever encountered including my parents. We keep Jesus in everything we do. He is an honorable man who fears the Lord. He is humble, respectful and treats me like a queen. It feels great to know that he chose me.

Over the next 5 years we built a great foundation based on loving God, mutual respect, and communication. He is disciplined when it comes to spending. I learned that I don't need everything I see. I now give to the poor and donate my time in community awareness. I am employed at a women's shelter advocating against domestic violence which provides a platform for public speaking to promote healthy relationships, safe sex, and birth control.

Travis encouraged me to take classes at Mercer County Community College where I earned a Liberal Arts Degree and transferred my credits to Rutgers where I am working to obtain a Bachelor's Degree in Counseling/Women's Studies. I always thank God for opportunities and for my experiences. I do what I do for the glory of God who gets all the credit. I now understand my Assignment.

Mookie and Evan invited us to dinner at Delta's. They also invited us to Sunday service at their new church. After all the laughs, dinner and dessert, the waiters stood around as Travis got down on one knee and proposed! I gladly gave him a tearful emphatic 'YES!' I had sworn off men times in my life, before and after jumping from man to man.

On a bright September Sunday morning, we got dressed and waited for Mookie and Evan to take us to service. Evan got out of the car to open the door for us and hugged me tight. I was happy for them; they were a cute couple. When we pulled off, I saw Mommy's red robin flying just ahead of us.

As we entered Hopewell A.M.E. Baptist Church, they were praising the Lord with song. It felt good to be there. I raised my hands and thanked Him for allowing me to be in the sanctuary. Many people welcomed us, including a big breasted woman that looked vaguely familiar. She grabbed me and said "Praise God! Thank you Jesus! Do you remember me?" I said, "I do!" She hustled me to the front of the church just as my Father's Uncle Reverend Marshall came out in a black robe.

He began to preach, but stopped in mid-sentence. "Well praise the Lord, daughter, please come up and introduce yourself, come on up!" I gladly stood up for the Glory of God. As he handed me the mic, I hugged him whimpering, "Thank you, so much." As I turned to the congregation, I silently prayed, 'Lord, please speak through me and let my words reflect my heart.'

"Good morning Saints, I'm Missy. I come before you to testify to the goodness of the Lord and how he saved a wretch like me. I was lost, literally." The church said "Yeah!" I continued, "I was a worldly mess! I was carnal minded. The devil had a good hold on me! I lost my way and now I'm free!" The church said, "Testify!" I began to cry, "Lord, I just want to say thank you. Thank you! You brought me a mighty long way."

I'm standing here to tell you today that I am a witness! A witness to the goodness of the Lord! Every step of my life I would live for that day. Now, with humility, I realize that is all He asks of each of us in Matthew 6:34. Jesus cannot use you unless you are fully broken. And I've been broken as low as you can go. I lost my child and my Mother on the same day! I lost my freedom and my family in the same week! I got good news for you church, a 'Little Bird' told me that you can be free from the bonds of this world! Now I follow God, not man! He blessed me with a new heart, a whole new loving family, a beautiful new mate who doesn't care about my past!

The good Lord showed me that, after this...I don't have to be alone! After this..., I can rest in the finished works of Almighty Jesus Christ! After this..., I don't have to be afraid to fail! After this..., I can forgive myself! After this..., I can love my enemies! After this..., I can be used by Him and not man! I'm so grateful today that I'm not dead! And I'll never stop praising His name!"

The Lord put a song in my heart that truly reflected my life and as I began to sing the choir joined in and the band played.

"Amazing Grace, how sweet the sound, that saved a wretch like me!"

The End

About The Author

T. E. Williams is a married mother of 4 adult children born and raised in Trenton, New Jersey. A natural born writer, Mrs. Williams aspires to encourage people with thought-provoking works of fiction which celebrate avenues of adversity and stumbling blocks we all encounter. Her hope is to raise consciousness and to inspire readers from all backgrounds to avoid the pitfalls and stay on the path laid out for you. She was inspired to write 'After This...!' after going through most of what the character Missy encountered. She hopes you will continue to support her in her effort by also reading, 'If Only...' 'For Now...' and 'After All...' Mrs. Williams has also written *Flawless*, a Christian stage play for teens which has been converted to paperback. Her life motto is, 'The World is Bigger Than Your Neighborhood'. 'After This...' is her first work but has been republished as a 2nd Edition. Visit IreeSky.com. T. E. Williams is a Born Again Christian and welcomes all audiences.